HOW
DROOFUS THE DRAGON
LOST HIS HEAD

written and illustrated by BILL PEET

Houghton Mifflin Company Boston

The Grand Spring Festival in this book is also a birthday party for my wife Margaret and my grandson Timothy, who were both born on the eighth day of April. A beautiful coincidence.

All rights reserved. For information about permission to reproduce selections from this book, write to Permissions, Houghton Mifflin Company, 215 Park Avenue South, New York, New York 10003.

Printed in the United States of America

WOZ   20   19

ISBN 0-395-15085-X Reinforced Edition
ISBN 0-395-34066-7 Sandpiper Paperbound Edition

Once upon a time there lived a family of dragons. They were a horrible bunch of beasts who traveled about from country to country stirring up trouble wherever they went.

One day on a trip to some faraway land the dragon family flew into a dense fog, and Droofus, the youngest of the dragons, lost track of the others.

Droofus kept circling about in the endless gray cloud, calling and calling in a squeeky small voice until at last he was too weary to flap his wings.

Then the little dragon gave up and went gliding down to land on a mountainside and crawled into a cave where he curled up in a corner to sleep for the night.

Droofus awoke the next morning feeling very lonely and ever so hungry. So he left his cave to find something for breakfast. Droofus was just four years old, and at that age dragons feed on small things like grasshoppers and beetles. As he was searching the tall grass near the cave he came across a grasshopper struggling helplessly in a spider web.

The spider was all set to pounce when suddenly Droofus snatched the grasshopper out of the web.

For a long while Droofus held the grasshopper by one leg wondering what to do. How could he eat someone just after saving his life? It didn't seem right, so he finally set the grasshopper free.

After that Droofus gave up eating grasshoppers and beetles and all other things that hopped or crept or crawled. As much as he disliked it the young dragon took to eating grass.

"It tastes awful," he said after one mouthful, "but I'll just have to get used to it." And sure enough, the more grass he ate the better he liked it. Pretty soon Droofus found the grass so tasty he was stuffing it down by the fistful.

And in a surprisingly short time the grass-eating dragon grew into a
giant of a monster, a huge scaly brute with a long pointed tail and big
leathery bat wings.

"There's too much of me now," grumbled Droofus. "I'm one big
overgrown lunk with nothing to do but eat and sleep." Then he re-
membered his wings. He hadn't been on a flight since he was four
years old, the day he was lost in the fog.

"Flying might be fun for a change," he said, and spreading his
wings he sailed up through the pines, then on out over the countryside.

It was a perfect day for flying, so sunny and clear he could make out every haystack that dotted the fields far below. He could see cows in the meadow, ducks in a pond, and a cart traveling along a yellow ribbon of a road past the farmhouses.

Farther on there were more roads and more houses — great clusters of houses with a castle towering above the rooftops. It was the castle of the king, and the king was out on a balcony to enjoy the beautiful morning.

"Great Gazootikens!" he cried, when he caught sight of Droofus. "A dragon! A whopper of a dragon!"

And the king watched in amazement until the dragon had sailed away to disappear in the forest high on the mountainside.

"What a marvelous thing it would be," he said, "to have that giant dragon's head on the wall of the great hall." And the king offered a reward of a hundred golden quadrooples for the dragon's head, which was a lot of money in those days.

That same afternoon every brave knight in the kingdom rode up the mountainside in search of the giant dragon.

Droofus was resting against a tree when the "clumpity clump" of horses hoofs and the "clankity clank" of armor reached his ears.

The two-ton dragon was much too weary from his sightseeing trip to go flying again, so he scurried back into his cave to hide.

The knights were looking for a cave with bones scattered about the entrance, but if they had gone all the way into one of them they would have seen Droofus.

After one peek into Droofus' cave they hurried on up the mountain-side, peeking into all the other caves as they went. The knights searched for months, peeking into hundreds of caves, but not one of them had the look of a dragon's cave. So at last they gave up in despair.

The dragon's hideout would have remained a mystery if a lamb hadn't gone astray one evening. The lamb had wandered into the pine forest on the mountainside, and before long a farm boy came looking for her. Lighting the way with a lantern, the boy followed the lamb's trail. Small bits of wool had caught on the brambles here and there. When he came to a cave he raised his lantern to peer inside.

At first there seemed to be nothing in the cave but rabbits, then farther back in the dark he spied a small white blob. It was the lamb curled up beside a scaly, pointed dragon's tail. And looming up to the roof of the cave was the rest of the dragon, sound asleep and snoring.

"Here, Flossy! Come on, Flossy," the boy called softly, careful not to awaken the dragon. The lamb finally raised her head, then hopped to her feet and came trotting out of the cave. And the boy and the lamb went scampering away through the forest.

Halfway down the mountain they met the boy's father and he was very angry.

"How many times must I warn you," he growled, "to stay out of the woods after dark."

"But I had to find Flossy," said the boy, "and you'd never guess where. She was sleeping in a cave with a dragon."

"A d-d-dragon!" stammered his father. "Are-are you sure?"

"A giant of a dragon!" said the boy.

"Why, son, did you know there's a reward for his head? A hundred gold quadrooples! The king's knights have been searching the mountain for months. If you lead the knights to his cave I'm sure you will get at least part of the reward."

"I can't do that," said the boy. "If he wouldn't hurt my lamb then he must be a good dragon. So I'll never tell anyone where he lives."

With nothing to worry about and so little to do, life was getting dull for Droofus, and he decided a change of scenery might help. One day he said good-bye to his cave and took off on a trip to most anywhere. However, he picked the very worst day for flying, and before he knew it Droofus was caught in a storm.

He wheeled around to head back for his cave—but too late. The fierce wind twisted his neck and tail and ripped at his wings and sent him tumbling backward into the clouds.

The dragon battled the storm until his wings were tattered to shreds. Then, helpless as a butterfly, he went whirling down out of the clouds to land with an earth shaking "Ker-whump" far out in a field.

Droofus was so badly battered and bruised he couldn't move. He was one big hurt from the point on his tail to the spikes on his nose. And he lay there sprawled out in the field while the storm went thundering away over the mountains.

Then he heard someone shouting, "It's the dragon! The big dragon! I saw him fall!" And pretty soon a small boy came running across the field, followed by a man and a woman. It was the same boy who had found his lamb in the dragon's cave.

"It's him all right," said the boy, after one look at Droofus.
"He appears to be dead," said his father.
"What a pitiful big thing," said his mother.

"But he's not dead," cried the boy. "He just blinked an eye!"

"I can blink an eye," groaned Droofus, "but that's all. I'm just about done for."

"Are you going to tell the king," the boy asked his father, "and collect the hundred quadrooples?"

"You found him, son. So that's for you to decide."

"He's a good dragon," said the boy, "and if I take good care of him he might get well."

Droofus was covered with a strawstack to keep him from chilling during the night. And every day the boy brought him bunches of fresh grass and a tub of fresh water. And every day the dragon felt a bit better.

"What makes your father so sad?" asked Droofus one day.

"Because we're so poor," said the boy. "And the reason we are poor is because of all these big rocks. They take up so much room there's not much land left to grow anything. We've tried every which way to get rid of them. But with everyone on the farm all pulling and pushing at once we can't budge even one of the rocks."

"That is enough to make anyone sad," sighed Droofus.

Early one morning, long before the first rooster crow, Droofus burst out of the strawstack feeling as fit as ever and just as good as new, except for his wings.

They were still so badly tattered they were useless. But the wings didn't matter. After that awful crash landing Droofus was through with flying. Besides, he had better things to do.

Seizing the nearest boulder in his powerful claws he jerked it off the ground, then carried it away to the far end of the field where he dropped it "Ker-blump!"

"That was easy," said Droofus. The next time he carried three rocks, then four and five, stacking them all into one pile. When the poor farmer stepped out of the door of his cottage that morning the land was half cleared, and he let out a "Whoop!" that could be heard for a mile.

"I told you he was a good dragon," said the boy.

"He's a great dragon!" cried his father, tossing his hat high in the air.

By noontime Droofus had piled every last rock into one big pyramid. At last the land was clear, and the happy farmer hitched his donkey to a plow and set out across the field.

"If that's what you call plowing," said the dragon, "I can do that too."

Jabbing his pointed tail deep into the ground, Droofus went trotting along, leaving a deep furrow, pulling up the weeds and eating them as he went.

After the plowing was done he helped plant the wheat. He hauled logs from the forest, and using his long jagged tail for a saw he cut enough firewood in one day to last the whole winter. When he ran out of things to do he stood in the wheatfield with his great arms outstretched serving as a very fine scarecrow.

"He's worth a lot more than a hundred quadrooples," said the happy farmer. "He's worth a thousand."

But the happiest of all was Droofus. At last he had become something useful, not just a big lunk of a thing. He no longer worried about the king's knights coming after him. The farm was so far out in the country hardly anyone knew it was there.

The only one to worry about was an old sheepherder who lived somewhere back in the hills. Once every spring the man drove his ox-cart over the bumpy road that ran past the farm on his way to the village to market his wool. The bad-tempered old fellow could be heard shouting at his oxen long before he passed by the farm. So there was plenty of time for Droofus to slip out of sight behind the barn.

But one spring day as the oxcart passed by, Droofus was careless and left his long pointed tail sticking out. The old sheepherder knew very well that such a tail could only belong to a dragon. When he reached the village late in the day the old fellow went straight to the castle to tell the king.

The next day the king and all his knights came riding up the road
to the farm on their great war horses, armed with swords and lances.

Droofus knew there was no use hiding. They had heard he was there or they wouldn't have come. So he stood there in the field while the farmer and his son ran out to meet them.

"We've come for the dragon," said the king, "and here's your reward of a hundred golden quadrooples."

"I don't want the reward," said the farmer. "The dragon's not for sale."

"I must have his head," said the king, "so please stand aside."

"But he's a good dragon," said the boy. "He's as tame as a kitten. He even sleeps by my bed every night."

"Look here, boy," growled the king, "I've got no time for tom-foolery."

"Oh, I didn't mean all of him," said the boy. "Only his head sleeps by my bed. He sticks his neck through the window and the rest of him stays outside."

"Well now, son, that's a bit more like it," said the king. "In fact, that gives me an idea. A grand idea! I'll borrow your dragon just for special occasions, and I'll pay you twenty quadrooples each time. What do you say to that?"

"It's up to the dragon," said the boy.

"Make it thirty quadrooples," said Droofus.

"Then thirty it is," said the king.

Droofus made his first visit to the king's castle on the eighth day of April, the day of the Grand Spring Festival. People came from miles around, crowding into the great hall, which was splendorously bedecked with banners and streamers and festoons of flowers. High up on the wall a giant of a dragon's head appeared through an elegant window framed in gold. A happy, smiling dragon's head that brought cries of surprise and squeals of delight and sent the crowd into a jolly frolicsome mood. Soon they were all singing and dancing to the music of trumpets and flutes and the Spring Festival was going full tilt.

The dragon was so carried away by all the merriment he suddenly burst into song with a booming, earsplitting voice that rocked the rafters and drowned out all the trumpets and flutes before he finally caught himself. In all the excitement Droofus the Dragon lost his head—but only for a moment.